Navigating Through Life

Frill's story

RICHARD AKINDEJI

Special thanks to
my grade 4 teacher Mme Boyce,
my friend Felix
and my dad for inspiring me to write this book.

Praise for *Navigating Through Life*

"Navigating Through Life: Frill's Story by Richard Akindeji is a remarkable blend of creativity, emotional depth, and youthful brilliance. This inspiring narrative transcends age, exploring perseverance, friendship, purpose, and redemption through the eyes of a gifted ten-year-old author. Akindeji's storytelling is both refreshing and profound. This is a testament that greatness begins with vision and courage. This compelling journey reminds us that resilience, determination and heart can turn life's storms into our greatest victories. A must-read masterpiece."

—Moses Mogbolu
Licensed REALTOR® and The Marketing Guru

"Navigating Through Life: Frill's Story is an inspiring, youth-friendly narrative about perseverance, friendship, and overcoming adversity. The story's relatable characters and engaging plot make it ideal for middle-grade readers, especially those interested in careers, teamwork, and personal growth. The writing is clear and accessible, with positive messages throughout. To reach the

right audience, it is advisable to promote it in schools, libraries, and youth organizations, and to highlight its themes of resilience and empathy.
—**Phillips Adewuyi** (FCA)

"*Navigating Through Life* is a thoughtful and imaginative story that showcases remarkable creativity and emotional depth for such a young author. The book traces Frill's journey through friendship, challenges, personal growth, and forgiveness. Richard's writing is engaging, clear, and full of meaningful lessons on courage, kindness, and perseverance. This is a beautiful and inspiring work that reflects both emerging talent and maturity, and it will speak to readers of all ages."
—**Folarin Williams**
Pastor, The Redeemed Christian Church of God, Pavilion of Redemption

"This is a wonderful and creative story for a Grade 5 student! Richard shows great imagination and organization as he takes readers on Frill's journey from childhood dreams to discovering his passion to help others. The story is full of emotion and shows a strong sense of perseverance and friendship. It's impressive how Richard makes us feel for the characters, drawing us in and helping us empathize with their struggles. This is a heartfelt story for someone of any age!"
—**Sarah McMullin**
Principal, Seaside Park Elementary

"Frill and Jim showed us how to be resilient in tough times as well as how to forgive; two very important life lessons. Thank you, Richard, for illustrating that we (paramedics) are human too! Looking forward to Part 2!"
—**Christopher Oakley**
Operations Manager
Primary Care Paramedic
Ambulance New Brunswick

Hi, my name is Frill. I live in Fredericton and I have a special story to tell you. It all started on a wet afternoon when it was raining heavily outside. I was around 7 years old at the time.

My mother, Sarah, was a nurse and she worked at the hospital till 11 pm. I didn't like that because I would have to spend the whole day with Dad who was working from home.

I would normally bug him all day, but I felt different today. So, I got one of the magazines on the table. It was all about jobs with a bit of sports and the latest news; I loved all the sections about jobs and sports. Then I came across a job recommendation which said, 'Love tech and a good salary cap? Apply now at AEA!'

I was wondering why Dad didn't apply for the job. It was a good deal plus he was good at tech. I was also trying to figure out what AEA meant. So, I went over to him to ask in a middle of a call. After I spoke, he let out a big sigh, meaning he was very tired and was annoyed.

So, I let him finish the call, but it ended almost immediately. ''Yes, I am listening,'' he said.

I asked him what AEA meant. He stood up straight from his chair, surprised I knew the word, but he didn't really ask how, so he said, ''Apex Engineering Association,'' in a grumpy voice.

I left, knowing it was for the best.

As the years went by, I was the top student in all my classes. I also received many opportunities in school for when I was in university. What made me be the best student in all my classes? It was the motivation of having a good job in the future.

Twelve years later I was 19 and in university, studying tech engineering which I was not really into. One night, alone in my apartment, I thought about my future. I thought about how the job I chose would affect my life, so I started looking for better opportunities.

Out of all of the jobs, two stood out the most, which was either being a paramedic or being a construction worker.

I was more into being a paramedic than a construction worker, so I studied about paramedics. Eventually I got into the APMA, which is a medical school.

I told my mom about it; she sounded so happy but also tired because she was still working at the hospital. And Dad had gone for the job I recommended to him when I was 7.

I was very nervous on my first day at APMA (Apex Medical Association) because there were so many people. When the class started, we were all separated into the groups we would be in till the end of our medical journey. I was assigned to group five which had ten boys and eight girls in total.

We took our seats at our desks. After we all got settled, we had to introduce ourselves.

I was beside someone named Jimmy Morin, but most people just called him Jim.

Jim was really nice and loved fire trucks so it was a perfect match.

After that, we had to learn some complicated facts we needed to know when we got out into the real world. After our first year of APMA, I was amazed I had learned so many things and that I was also the top of my class.

For our second year, things went downhill a lot. First, Jim doesn't trust me anymore because we'd had an incident in class. Jim got a question wrong and I answered impolitely, which made him furious, so he no longer talked to me about anything. Instead, he talked with the person I disliked the most in our class ... Jermey.

Jermey was a really annoying and selfish guy; he liked gossiping a lot about people, especially if it wasn't his business.

So, I didn't really have friends but Mom said Jim would eventually forgive me and I should just focus on my classes.

Finally it was year three, which meant that after this year we were cleared for being nurses, doctors, or paramedics. Another great thing was that Jim was finally my friend again. He was upset with Jermey because he trusted Jermey with personal information about his family, and Jermey promised he wouldn't tell anyone. But everyone knew Jermey and he told the whole school.

When Jim confronted Jermey, he told him, ''Well I guess you shouldn't have trusted me sucker.''

Jim was very sorry when he came back to me, so we were friends again and everyone had forgotten what Jermey said about his family.

The final day of APMA arrived and everyone was so happy, except Jermey. He was telling everyone in the school, including Jim and me, that "I'm going to miss bullying you a lot suckers."

Everyone ignored him but Jim had had enough of everything, and said, ''I am tired of you always bullying people. Can't you just quit it!''

Jermey remained silent and just nodded and left. "That should give him a taste of his own medicine," said Jim.

Then Jim and I had a chat about which hospital we were planning to go to.

Jim gave a firm answer: ''ARH''. I was shocked he said that because it was almost impossible to get in there as it was Fredericton's national hospital ARH means (Apex Regional Hospital).

I was thinking it wasn't going to happen. We surely wouldn't make it and be a part of their paramedic squad, but still he encouraged me to apply.

A week later, we got a call from ARH saying they would love it if both Jim and I came to work as paramedics for them. Jim was in disbelief that we had made it into ARH but it was real and we had to prepare.

It was three days till we worked our first shift in ARH, so we really had to work to get ourselves ready. I would be driving the ambulance while Jim would do all the check-ups because I just liked sitting in front enjoying the sweet vehicle we were going to get. Jim was more the type of guy who loved talking to people, even if they were strangers.

Finally the day came, our first day at ARH as paramedics. It was pretty cool because we got to go in where all the staff, including the paramedics come in. We also got to meet our ambulance.

This was ambulance number 583 with its special patterns to say to keep a distance of 30 ft (which equals 360 inches) away. We also got to meet our medic chief, a position which only ARH has.

Our chief was named Dan; he was really nice and was actually a firefighter. He had been a paramedic when he was about our age, which was fantastic because he knew everything we needed to know as paramedics.

I learned how to start the engine and Jim got to learn tips from Chief. We then got our gear on—which I was sweating in, Jim too—and were sitting down on the bench for paramedics.

Thirty minutes went by and there was a call for a breathing difficulty. The responder at her desk said, "Any medics available for call 259?" I responded on my radio, "Yes, medics 583 are available for the call."

The responder gave us the address and said that they sounded in pain so we should hurry. Immediately the responder finished, we got up and jogged up to the ambulance which was really clean.

I turned on the engine while Jim got in the back and we zoomed off to the emergency. Upon our arrival, we saw a woman waving her hands at us. She looked very worried.

I parked our ambulance in their driveway while Jim got our medical box for checking the patient's vitals. When we got in, we saw a young boy of about 12 years old with a very serious breathing problem.

Jim asked when it happened and what the child was doing, while I was examining vitals. His blood pressure was extremely high, which was not good at all. We told them that he must be taken to the hospital immediately. His mom agreed but the young fellow just kept breathing faster and faster.

It took about five minutes to get to the hospital and when we got there, he was immediately taken to the ER (Emergency Room).

After our first rescue, Chief called us into his office for an important meeting. When we got there, we saw two other men named Tom and Jeff, who were the owners of ARH.

They were very happy to meet us and had heard about our first rescue from our first shift. They said we should discuss how much we would get paid for being paramedics at ARH. I first thought we could do it for free but my parents would have not approved of that, and we would have to make money, so we decided that $6,000 per month would be a good deal.

We didn't get any more calls and got to go home for the night. "Today was awesome," said Jim happily.

Jim and I, along with our parents, decided he should share my apartment because it had two bedrooms and it was closer to the hospital. When we got home from work, we were usually tired and this way we could just go to bed.

Three months later, Jim and I had saved 10,000 Canadian dollars each from being paramedics at ARH. But something bad happened to me that nearly caused me to lose my job.

First, we got a call that someone had broken their leg in an MABL game (Major Apex Basketball League), which was something serious we had to attend to.

We had our patient loaded up in the back of the ambulance as usual. The only problem was that the cars weren't moving and when I honked at them some of them didn't move. So I sped up the ambulance and almost hit someone, making our patient in much discomfort and made a mess with the tools in the back.

ARH
583
KEEP A DISTANCE O
30 FT

When we got to the hospital, Dan gave me a glare because obviously he had heard about what happened. He said he wanted to talk to me in his office immediately.

He said I might lose my spot with ARH because there were other people wanting it more and that I had almost made things worse for that poor boy. I told him this had been my only mistake.

But he didn't care. He said I shouldn't come to work for three weeks and then they would have a response for me. But I asked who would drive Jim if I was away? The chief said, "You don't have to worry about Jim, just worry about yourself," and that was the end of the conversation.

I came back to my apartment furious but later calmed down. I was worried for Jim. A few hours later, Jim was done for the day and came home very worried. He asked, "Where were you?! I was looking all over for you, but Chief said you needed some time off for the day."

I knew the chief wouldn't tell Jim that I was about to lose my job, and plus he might just also make Jim lose his job too. I was angry so I didn't answer when he spoke, I just went to my room.

I didn't get called for one week, and I was getting worried. Then two weeks and eventually three went by, and still no response.

It was at this point I knew it was over. I was never getting called again. Then a miracle happened. On Friday the fifth of October, the ARH called me saying they needed me back.

I was filled with joy I could resume my medical journey as a paramedic for ARH with Jim. When I got to the station everyone was happy to see me again except the chief because he still hadn't forgotten about my last call.

We then got a call about a little girl who had gotten serious food poisoning at Frank's Chicken and Beef after eating their newest chicken beef burger wrap. Jim and I immediately got in our ambulance and drove to Frank's Chicken and Beef where the patient was.

When we arrived, everyone started to stare at us because it wasn't every day you see two paramedics coming to help a child who has gotten food poisoning at Frank's Chicken and Beef eating their newest chicken beef burger.

Jim asked the patient's parents questions to get more understanding of the situation while I checked her vitals.

As Jim and the parents were deciding on going to the hospital, suddenly the patient's heartbeat slowed down. I immediately tugged Jim's arm saying we might lose her, knowing that when your partner tugged your arm it was time for serious action.

We told them she needed to get to the hospital ASAP or we might lose her. Just saying that made me feel nervous as I was driving the ambulance and I knew this little girl's life being saved could depend on how fast I drove.

When we finally arrived at the hospital with the girl, we put her on the stretcher and got her to the ER.

I could see on the chief's face that, if the little girl had died, I would be done for and so would Jim. When we went home, I had this weird feeling I did something wrong or like there was something I could have done for the girl but I just didn't do it.

The next morning Jim and I arrived at the hospital only to find that the chief was waiting outside for us.

I thought, *Oh no, the little girl died and now I am fired,* but the real reason was because … The little girl's parents wanted to thank us for saving their daughter.

I was surprised to hear that," It's our pleasure." Said Jim , and the parents thanked us a few more times before they went to go back and see their child.

Suddenly, Chief coughed and said, "I don't know how you two did it, but I have no choice but to put you both in The Hall of Medical." (This was similar to The Hall of Fame.)

I was in shock because only five paramedics had made it there: Bobby Vince Jr, Albert Fin, Kyle Boyce, Paul Harden and Edward Stuward.

I couldn't believe Frill Strom and Jimmy Morin were now the sixth and seventh paramedics to be in The Hall of Medical.

We were also able to be paid more so we got to talking and decided on 9,000 dollars per month. That was the highest anyone in ARH had been paid in a decade.

Jim and I gladly accepted the offer.

Three years later Jim and I had earned 324,000 Canadian dollars—648,000 in total between us, which was more than enough.

Then my parents called me and said I had a little brother. I was in shock that I had a little brother; they told me he was about 9 months old.

I asked why they hadn't told me before. What they said made me chuckle because they said, ''You were busy."

I laughed with joy to hear that, and to hear my little brother who was trying to say hi to me.

Then the worst thing ever happened in my life.

HALL OF MEDICAL

BOBBY VINCE JR.

ALBERT FIN

EDWARD STUWARD

PAUL HARDEN

KYLE BOYCE

JIMMY MORIN

FRILL STORM

It was a nice Sunday at the ARH. Out of nowhere my mom called me. I hesitated to pick up the call but told Jim I needed to use the bathroom.

All he said was okay and hurry up because a call could come in at any time, so I went to the men's bathroom and asked my mom why she was calling me.

She spoke very fast saying my little brother's heart was failing him. I asked how they knew that because they didn't have the right tools to tell; I forgot I gave them a vitals box so they could check each other's vitals to check everyone was healthy.

After I heard that, I rushed out of the bathroom and was about to tell Jim but he said we had a call—a 9-month-old kid who is having heart problems.

Immediately Jim finished I told him this boy was my younger brother. Jim said there was no time to waste.

Upon our arrival, I was getting memories of when I was staring at the window on that rainy day looking at the newspaper telling Dad about the job recommendation for AEA but quickly snapped out of it.

When we got inside, I remembered the sweet smell of this home when I was still living there, and then I saw the worst thing possible in my life. My little brother was unconscious on the floor in my dad's arms.

I said to myself this was not possible, that I would not let my little brother die like this.

We got him into the ambulance and I went over the speed limit because I had to. Jim kept saying his heartbeat was failing.

The more he said that the faster I went, and we got there in record time, breaking one minute.

When Chief saw us, he was shocked to see me with my parents. I told him what had happened while Jim was getting my brother into the hospital.

But by that time, it was too late.

The next thing I knew my parents had appeared and were crying. It was at that moment I realised the worst had happened.

My little brother had died.

When I heard that, I didn't say another word.

I just left the hospital as my parents mourned and Jim tried to convince me to stay; that we could talk it out.

I went home, thinking about my life and how I had just ruined it.

Because of me my little brother's life had ended.

In the span of a week, I received more than 50 calls from my parents; I barely ate anything the whole time. Then I noticed Jim wasn't in the apartment very often. I just thought he'd gone shopping or was hanging out with some of his other friends.

But that wasn't the case, the real truth was he was still working as a paramedic at ARH.

When I discovered that I was raging mad at him, and when he got home, we had a heated argument which ended in Jim moving out of my apartment. He went to rent his own apartment away from mine.

After the argument, I thought about my life and how it had started as good as it could have possibly been and how now it was at the worst part.

And even worse—my biggest fear came true.

Being alone.

Having no one beside me.

And only one person was to blame.

Life was very hard.

Very, very hard.

And very unfair.

I was so hurt, I didn't eat for 13 hours that day.

Then, someone called me.

It was the Chief. When I answered I just said, ''I already know what you're going to say, Chief.''

Chief said, ''Really?''

''Yeah, that I am fired,'' I replied.

Then he said, ''Your mom told me about your whole medical journey, about how you met Jim. How Jermey bullied everyone. Frill, you have been through a lot, and when I say a lot, I mean *a lot*.''

''But why should I be the one who says your dreams are over,'' he continued, "many people can say your dreams are over. But it's you yourself who knows if it's over.'

''So, Frill, what I have been trying to say is that you're not fired.''

When Chief said that I was speechless.

I asked if he was joking, but he said no.

I then asked Chief who my partner for our calls would be, and he said the same person that I had started with: Jimmy Morin.

I told him what had happened between Jim and me and that I didn't know where he was.

Chief told me to call his number, so I did 25 times and there was still no response. But then I remembered something. I thought I knew where Jim was.

After the call ended, I went into Jim's room. It was empty with nothing except a little piece of paper that had an address on it.

I'd seen it before when Jim was moving out but I had been too angry to pick it up.

The address said: 30 St Roses Drive, Apartment 11.

Now I knew where to look for Jim.

I went outside and got into a Vet taxi. I told the driver named Gabe to go to 30 St Roses Drive, Apartment 11.

Once we got there, I paid Gabe 14 Canadian dollars for the ride. After he left, I found apartment 11 and rang the doorbell.

When the door opened, Jim was smiling which was good, until he saw my face, then his became annoyed.

He was about to slam the door but I told him I was very sorry and just because I didn't want to go to ARH for a while, it didn't mean he couldn't. "Because you are the one who decides if you want to work or not."

Then Jim and I got a little teary and hugged it out. I told him why I was there and that Chief hadn't fired me.

Eventually, when I came home, I immediately asked Chief if Jim and I could come into work tomorrow.

But Chief said Jim and I needed a break, then both of us could come and work again after a week.

I was fine with that and was happy my friendship was back to normal.

One week later, I called Jim because he said he liked his apartment so we would have to go to work separately.

JIMMY
FRILL

I then left my apartment to go to the hospital. When I arrived, everyone was cheering for me; even Chief gave me a big smile.

However, Jim came up behind me and told me we had a call to get to.

I got into my uniform, hopped in the ambulance and we were about to drive off to our next rescue.

However, Chief said no, that Jim and I were going on a different mission. A mission that could possibly be the most amazing opportunity in our medical career.

He told us the QIA had said to Tom and Jeff that they were looking for two paramedics to be on stand-by for the Q1 race at Circuit D'Oasis located in Montreal Quebec.

Jeff was about to say nobody was available, but Tom said that their best medics, Frill Strom and Jimmy Morin, could come on standby.

After that, QIA and Tom made an agreement.

Jeff was questioning if he should have really put Jim and me in there, as he knew what just happened with my family.

But Tom trusted that I could do it.

We also had to meet with them to ensure that if anything went wrong, we could call them and they would send help.

He also said, "This might be one of your biggest emergencies, if there is an accident. And you both have a long 8 hours and 1 minute drive if traffic is okay, so you better get going."

When Tom finished, Jim was more than excited.

He was so happy he would be one of the Q1 paramedics for the Circuit D'Oasis race and said we should be going as the race was starting in five days.

But Jim and I had a little problem.

We didn't own a car.

Now we get paid a lot, but Jim and I were still saving up until the right moment.

We told Chief about our problem and he said we could use our ambulance to get there. We had to talk to the head of transportation if we wanted to use it for our trip, however.

After Chief told us that we went over to Matt's desk. Matt was the head of transportation. We asked him if we could use the ambulance for the trip.

"Of course you can guys." He was clearly happy for us when he said it.

Now that we had our vehicle problem solved, we had another problem.

Where were we going to sleep?

Because I was not driving for 8 hours and 1 minute without some sleep. Jim said we could stop at the nearest hotel when I was tired.

Now the final problem was we couldn't go without food.

But I remembered my mom said she could pack some food for us for the road.

So, Jim and I got all the supplies we needed for our trip from Fredericton to Montreal.

… and we set off on our journey.

It had been an hour of driving and it was already 5pm. We still had 7 hours of driving left.

When it was 8 p.m. with 4 hours left of driving to get to Montreal, I got sleepy so I asked Jim where the nearest hotel was. He suggested, "The Highway Hotel."

I pulled up at the place and it looked nice, but when we entered we didn't see a lot of people there.

"That's because it's a three-star hotel," said Jim. But it was better than nothing.

We went to the counter to get a room for the night. The attendant at the desk was chewing gum, and was so rude because she said, "Like … are you guys dressing up, or is it just for Halloween?"

The date was February 29th, not October 31st!

So I told her we were paramedics, but she didn't listen.

Eventually, the manager walked by and saw what was happening.

He apologised and told the attendant to go home for the night, which she did, and the manager gave us room 35 on the 3rd floor.

I was still angry about the attendant, and Jim was confused as to why she thought it was Halloween.

We took an elevator to the third floor and when we got off the place looked beautiful.

We found our room, but we forgot to say to the manager Jim and I needed two rooms because each room only had one bed.

So, I made the journey all the way downstairs and asked the manager if we could get another room, please.

Because he was very nice, he gave me an extra room.

I went up to the third floor and gave Jim the keys to his room for the night.

Finally I got into my bed and instantly fell asleep.

The next day at 7 a.m., I decided that we should get going because the race was starting in 4 days and we were still 4 hours away from Montreal.

I headed downstairs and went to get something to eat.

When I saw the menu, I was not pleased.

The only thing they had for the morning was coffee and tea.

I picked tea because coffee has a very strong smell in my opinion, although that doesn't mean it was bad.

Eventually, Jim came downstairs and suggested we leave.

I quickly finished my tea, while Jim took his coffee and paid for the night we had stayed.

Then, we climbed into our ambulance and got on the road.

After driving for another 4 hours, we officially made it into Montreal, Quebec.

After driving for another 30 minutes, we saw it: Circuit D'Oasis .

When Jim saw this, he was in shock because as a kid Jim had always wanted to watch a live Q1 race in person.

Now he had the chance to.

But the race didn't start for 4 days.

So, I asked Jim where the closest hotel to the race track was.

He said, "L'hôtel-Chau Chateau."

Once we had arrived there, we saw none other than Jermey.

When I saw him I didn't really pay attention, but for Jim, it was a different story.

He even asked me if that really was him, but then Jermey got a glimpse of Jim and turned around and said, "Well well well. What do we have here? If it isn't my two least favourite people,

Frill and Jim. So, what brings you to Montreal? Are you here to watch me, the leading champion in Q1, beat the competition?"

Jim started to ask why he wasn't a paramedic.

Jermey gave a mean answer: "It's none of your business."

Jim wasn't happy, but he told me that we should go get a room. Eventually, we got a room on the 2nd floor, and this time it had two beds.

So, for the next four days, Jim and I stayed at the hotel, which also housed Jermey, who was apparently another Q1 racer.

The day finally came. The Circuit D'Oasis race at 2:00 p.m. sharp.

Jim was so excited until Jermey broke his happy bubble.

He said, "Well you guys are not going to enjoy the race because I am going to win it."

I ignored him, but as always Jim took it personally.

We left L'hôtel-Chau Chateau and drove to the racetrack, while Jermey got special transportation—he was being driven in a limousine.

When we got there, it was a full crowd.

You could feel the energy in the stadium.

Eventually, they were calling out the positions for the race, and surprisingly, Jermey was the race leader with 19 points.

We arrived at the place where all the track paramedics stay, and took a seat, as the race had started.

There were four laps of the 30-lap race left to go.

Out of nowhere, Jermey was in second place and Bob Griff had the lead.

Jermey came to the outside of a turn and tried to hit Bob's car, but Bob sped up and drove out of the way.

4 LAPS
TO GO

When that happened, Jermey tried to stay on track but he spun around and his car flipped over multiple times, finally, bursting into flames.

Straight away, they waved a red flag and stopped the race.

They then called on the paramedics to come to the site. Jim and I immediately hopped over the fence that had been set up for paramedics.

When we got to the crash area, Jim stopped.

He just stood there, looking at Jermey's car in flames.

I told him to move but he said we should just leave him there.

When he said that, I was shocked.

But I remembered what Jermey did to him in APMA.

I told him the past was the past. That it didn't matter what people did to you. You always have to forget it and move on.

Thankfully, Jim snapped out of it and moved to help Jermey who was trapped in a car of flames.

After the fire was put out, the firefighters used a claw to break up all the debris so they could get Jermey out of the car.

We then put him on the stretcher we brought over from the ambulance.

We loaded him in and rushed him to HDM (L'Hôpital De Montreal), where he was then taken to the ER. We then waited for him to wake up.

After a few hours, the doctor told me and Jim that Jermey would have to stay at the hospital for three days in order to fully recover from his accident.

I asked the doctor what type of injuries we were talking about, and he said, "Burns, dirty lungs and probably stroke."

JIMMY
FRILL

But a miracle happened—Jermey woke up.

When this happened I was so happy that he was alive … even Jim was.

Then Jermey asked why we had saved him and why we didn't let him die after all the things he had done to us.

Jim replied, using my quote: "The past is the past."

Jermey asked if we could forgive him, and Jim and I both said at the same time: "We forgave you a long time ago."

After we said that, Jermey broke down in tears and apologised.

The doctor said someone had to stay there with him, as he was not ready to be left alone.

Jim said that we could stay with him for the three days, as long as there was food, a bathroom and TV.

So, the doctor agreed Jim and I could stay and be with him until he recovered.

And I was glad he said that because those few days at the hospital with Jermey were the best.

The day finally came when Jermey was going to be discharged.

We walked out of the hospital, going to our ambulance, but Jermey said that he didn't want to continue racing anymore.

He said he wanted to join us and be a paramedic.

I told him, "It is you who decides when you are ready to stay or move on, so come on, what are you waiting for? We have to get back to Fredericton."

Jermey was delighted he could be a paramedic.

We then made the 8 hour and 1 minute journey back to Fredericton where Jermey said he wanted to work.

The next day, we asked Chief if Jermey could come work there as a paramedic too.

Chief said there wasn't enough room, but I pleaded if they could fit him in.

So, Tom and Jeff talked about it and agreed Jermey could join us as a paramedic if he was okay getting paid $6,000 per month, which was okay with him.

As we were preparing for any calls, Chief said since we'd done an amazing job, the three of us would be going around the world on different missions.

"This time you guys get your very own private jet with a pilot. Now get moving, because your next mission is in San Francisco."

Once we heard that, we immediately got ready for our flight around the world to not just save people but also to connect with lots of different people.

I am Frill Strom and that's my story.

Navigating Through Life 2 is coming soon!

APMA
APMA

About the Author

Hello, my name is Richard Akindeji. I am 10 years old and proud to be trilingual! I live in Saint John, NB, and I am currently a student at Seaside Park Elementary School.

When I'm not writing, you can usually find me enjoying sports. My favorites to play are hockey, basketball, baseball, and football. When it comes to watching, nothing beats the excitement of hockey and Formula 1 (F1)!

My hockey loyalties are with the San Jose Sharks, Seattle Kraken, Calgary Flames, and our own QMJHL team, the Saint John Sea Dogs. In F1, I root for the Alpine BWT and Red Bull Racing teams.

I also love music, and my favorite instrument to play is the piano. In school, my top subjects are Phys Ed, Math, and Science, but my favorite thing to do in my free time is reading and writing— which is why this book exists!

Thank you so much for reading the first book in this series. I hope you enjoyed it! Be on the lookout because *Navigating Through Life* is going to have sequels, and even some special editions, coming out soon!

www.ingramcontent.com/pod-product-compliance
Lightning Source LLC
Chambersburg PA
CBHW071014120726
47910CB00004B/1524